The Blue Kangaroo

by

Mary Jane Flynn, M.D.

Look for
Other Books by
Mary Jane Flynn, M.D.

The Lost & Found Puppy

If a Seahorse Wore a Saddle

I Thought I Heard a Tiger Roar

For Erin,
Meghan,
Sean,
Christopher,
and Killian

A blue kangaroo
has escaped
from the zoo!

He may hop past
your window –
THEN what will
you do?

You *COULD* try to catch him, but this clever fellow...

Might hide in a raincoat and hop by all YELLOW!

He knows many tricks to avoid being seen.

He might hide in some leaves, and then hop right by GREEN!

But one of the
tricks that he
likes best of all...

Is to bounce right
along in a big
ORANGE ball!

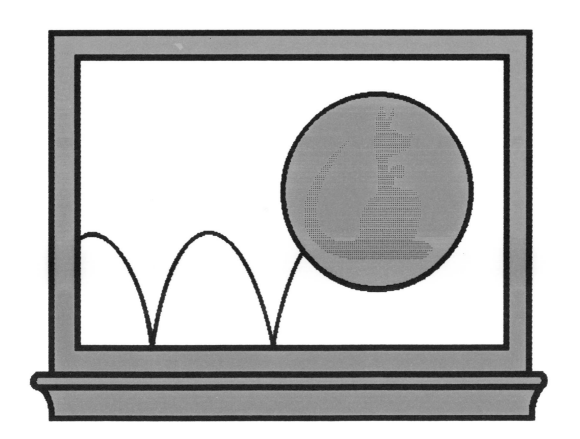

He once dressed
like Santa
and sat in a sled.

He fooled
EVERYBODY when
he drove by RED!

He likes to ride trains as they roar down the track –

With a big puff of smoke, he may rush by all BLACK!

This isn't a
GHOST hopping by
late at night –

It is only that
blue kangaroo
dressed in WHITE!

Now he'll say
a farewell
to his friends
at the zoo.

But I'm sure
you'll see more
of the blue
KANGAROO!

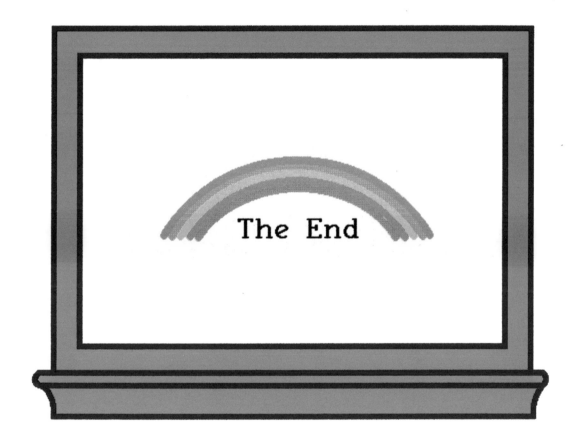